The Miracle of Vanessa Swan

Adventures of an Arctic Mermaid

"The meaning of life is to find your gift.
The purpose of life is to give it away."
-Pablo Picasso

Written & Illustrated by Laura Martindale Welch

This book is dedicated to my father God who placed this story in my heart
and to my daughter Vanessa, the best gift God ever gave us.

Just for fun...
find the hidden feather on each page.

ISBN: 978-1-64704-915-7 (paperback)
ISBN: 978-1-64704-916-4 (hardcover)
ISBN: 978-1-64704-917-1 (ebook)
ISBN: 978-1-64704-918-8 (audiobook)

The Miracle of Vanessa Swan
Copyright 2023 Laura Martindale Welch (Artistic i LLC)

Written & Hand Illustrated by Laura Martindale Welch
Illustrations are not a product of AI.

Artistic i LLC
First printing edition 2024

This book belongs to:

It was an answer to a prayer. A husband and wife had been praying for a child and she had finally arrived.
She was born at the bottom of the cool, deep Arctic Ocean within a kingdom of mermaids.

Admiring sea life circled the newborn with amazement. She was unlike any of the others. She was born with a crown of light and delicate wings that looked like those of a swan.
In celebration of her unique appearance, they named her Vanessa Swan.

As Vanessa grew up, she discovered her crown of light gave her the power to communicate with the sea animals. Unfortunately, when she tried to speak with them, they would avoid her.

At school, kids would say hurtful things and pluck her feathers to tease her. She tried hiding her wings using a jacket, a backpack, and even an umbrella. Nothing hid her wings, and covering them only made her look more ridiculous. At night, she would pray, "Please God, I just want to be normal like everyone else."

On Vanessa's tenth birthday, her parents surprised her with a seal pup she named Snowball. Snowball didn't avoid her or treat her differently, and the two of them became inseparable.

They loved playing hide-and-seek together, but they weren't very good at it. Vanessa's wings always gave her hiding spot away, and Snowball could only hold his breath for a few minutes before he had to go up for air. One day, Vanessa decided to follow him up to the surface.

Vanessa was amazed the moment she emerged from the water.
She spotted creatures with wings, just like hers, flying through
the air. "What are they?" she asked. Snowball replied, "They
are tundra swans and ivory gulls." Seeing them glide so easily
through the air gave her an idea.

"Don't do it! You might fall! You might get hurt!" Snowball cried.
Vanessa said, "If I don't try, I'll never know if I can."
Despite Snowball's warnings, she climbed an iceberg, stretched
out her wings, and felt them lift her into the air.

At first she felt wobbly, but with each flap of her wings she flew higher and steadier. Soon she was soaring gracefully alongside the birds. Like a kite without a string she sailed through the sky.

Vanessa opened her arms wide. She had never felt so free.
Maybe this was the world she was meant for.

She was dreaming about life outside the sea when she heard a
bird mocking her. The seagull said, "Ha! What is this – a flying fish?
I think you're lost! With a tail like that, you belong in the ocean!"
Vanessa stopped flapping her wings and allowed the birds to pass
her by. Slowly sinking through the sky, her heart felt broken.

Returning to the surface, she curled up in tears. Snowball said, "I wish I could've been there with you. I would have taught that bird a lesson!"

Overhearing them, a little puffin waddled over and offered her a new spring flower. "My name is Muffin. Why are you all upset?" Vanessa explained what had happened. Muffin said, "I can swim and fly too! Don't let that bird-brain make you feel bad." Vanessa was grateful for the puffin's kindness, but Muffin didn't understand.

The next day, Vanessa and Snowball had a swimming race. When Vanessa reached the finish line, she noticed something terrible: the sea was full of garbage! The seals and belugas were suffering because the plastic was making them sick or causing them to get tangled up. Vanessa knew she had to act fast to help them.

Vanessa stopped the sea animals from eating the plastic and untangled the others. Once they were feeling better, they noticed the garbage was still all around them. They were lost and needed a way out.

Vanessa had an idea. "Quickly, everyone come to the surface, I will find a way!" she said. With her powerful wings, she flew out of the water and floated above the maze of garbage. They followed her away from the trash to cleaner water.

The sea animals were grateful to Vanessa for saving them;
her wings had helped them escape. Vanessa tried to find
Snowball so they could return home. Before she could find
him, she heard sounds coming from a nearby fishing boat.
She knew to stay away from boats, yet she had to investigate.

Birds were trying to eat the fisherman's catch and getting caught in the net. She knew she had to save them too.

Vanessa dove into the water and swam to the net. Her powerful tail pushed her forward. The birds had made fun of her fishtail, but it gave her the power she needed. They knew she was their only hope.

Vanessa released the birds one by one. The last bird was the one that had teased her. "I'm so sorry. Will you forgive me?" the bird asked. "I already have," Vanessa replied as she freed him from the net.

On that day, everyone learned something valuable.
The birds and sea animals now knew that Vanessa's
differences were not weaknesses; they were strengths.
She was able to help them in ways that no one else could.

Vanessa began to see herself in a new way. She realized she didn't want to be normal. Her abilities gave her purpose. By using the gifts God had given her, she could make a difference in the world around her.

About the Author Laura Martindale Welch

Laura is a Fine Arts major who has been living in Charleston, SC for over 30 years. She resides with her husband Jason, daughter Vanessa, and their Maltese Picasso.
"I am a child of God, a wife, mother, artist, live wedding painter, and now author and illustrator. I am a continuous work in progress and always looking to go where God wants me next. This book was my next."

Thank you for reading The Miracle of Vanessa Swan!
If you would like to share this book with others:

👍 Like our Instagram page #artisticibooks
👍 Share on your social media
👍 Leave a review on Amazon

We would love to hear from you! Your support is a blessing.
To learn more, please scan the QR code below or
visit our website Artisticibooks.com

Scripture to Lock in Your Heart

"God has given each of you a gift from His great variety of spiritual gifts. Use them well to serve one another." 1 Peter 4:10-11

"Be kind and compassionate to one another, forgiving each other, just as Christ God forgave you." Ephesians 4:32

"But I tell you, love your enemies and pray for those who persecute you." Matthew 5:44

"But those who wait for the Lord shall renew their strength; they shall mount up with wings like eagles, they shall run and not be weary, they shall walk and not faint" Isaiah 40:31

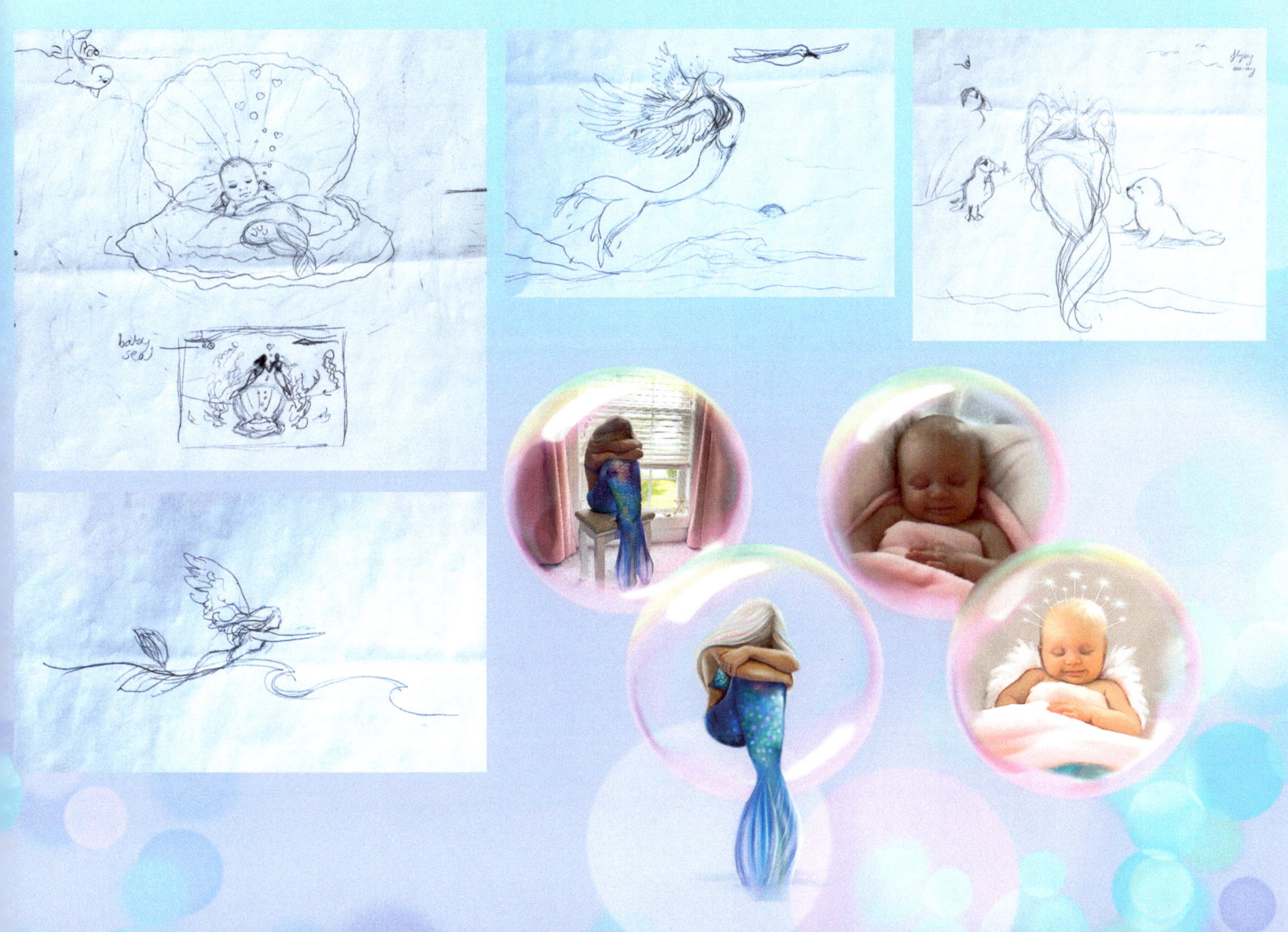